PRIVATE TICKL:

Written by Roger Bensaid
Illustrated by Robert Coveney

Published by New Generation Publishing in 2019

Copyright © Roger Bensaid 2019

First Edition

The author asserts the moral right under the Copyright, Designs and Patents Act 1988 to be identified as the author of this work.

All Rights reserved. No part of this publication may be reproduced, stored in a retrieval system or transmitted, in any form or by any means without the prior consent of the author, nor be otherwise circulated in any form of binding or cover other than that which it is published and without a similar condition being imposed on the subsequent purchaser.

ISBN: 978-1-78955-808-1

www.newgeneration-publishing.com

New Generation Publishing

This is the story of a little soldier boy called Private Tickles.

He is the youngest and newest soldier in the Toy Town Army.

Private Tickles was feeling just a little bit sad. He was so young and new, everybody seemed to give him jobs to do.

No sooner had he finished one job than somebody would give him another one. Everybody from General Basher to Corporal Careless bossed him about.

Noodle the cat tried to cheer him up.

'Tickles, peel the potatoes' said Corporal Cook.

Noodle just sat on a stool and cleaned her paws.

'Tickles, guard the gate' shouted Corporal Careless.

Tickles was too young to have a proper gun,
he was only allowed a big stick.

'Tickles, saddle my horse' said General Basher.

Tickles liked the General's horse, it was a very friendly horse called Tumbleweed.

'What are you doing now, Private Tickles?'
shouted Sergeant Major Bullhorn.

Poor Private Tickles got himself into such a mess and a muddle because he had so many jobs to do.
He really didn't know if he was coming or going.

'Tickles, get tidied up boy' shouted Sergeant Major Bullhorn. Tickles had so little time to keep himself neat and tidy that he was always in trouble with Sergeant Major Bullhorn but there was one job that Tickles didn't mind at all, in fact he quite enjoyed it and that was walking Bacon the dog.

Bacon the dog was Tickles best friend.

One day Tickles was getting ready to peel enough potatoes for the whole of the Toy Town Army. 'WOW!' he thought, 'I've never seen so many potatoes in all my life.'
Just then, he began to daydream......

'What I really need' he thought 'is someone or something to help me, ...hmmm, perhaps a little magic would do the trick'......

He waved his hands over the baskets of potatoes……'Potatoes, peel" he whispered. He felt his nose twitch and twitch until it built up into a big sneeze………….. ATISHOOOO!………….'PEEL' he shouted………..and they did.

'WOW!' thought Tickles, 'I wonder if it would work on the boots?' That afternoon he had to clean the boots for the entire Toy Town Army and the General's shoes as well. It was one of the hardest and longest jobs he had to do.

The boot room was always hot and smelly, his hands and fingernails always got filthy, his uniform got messy and the job seemed never-ending.

HE HATED IT

'Shoes and boots' he said, and waved his hands over his head and then over the boots and shoes. He felt his nose begin to tickle until, A - A - Atishoooo……'Shine' he shouted…………………..and they did.

Noodle was nowhere to be seen.

Suddenly Tickles began to feel a little bit strange, he didn't understand magic and was just a little bit afraid. 'Where did the magic come from?' he thought. 'Why did it choose me?' but most of all he didn't want the magic to go away.

He wished for an answer………..his nose began to tickle and then, ……..A - A - Atishoooo, he did such a big sneeze and there in front of him was……………The Wizard of the Lake. Tickles was amazed and very, very scared. The Wizard was always very, very serious and people always took great care not to upset him, just in case, but, when the Wizard saw it was Tickles who had summoned him, he just smiled.

The Wizard had seen how hard Tickles had to work every day with all of the jobs and duties he had to do, so, he had given him the magic to help him along.

Tickles was the youngest and newest soldier in the Toy Town Army and he was always given the work that no-one else wanted to do.

'Well" said the Wizard, 'I have seen you working so hard and I thought that a little magic would help you.'

'Thank you Mr Wizard" said Tickles and asked 'will the magic last'?

'That depends on you' the Wizard smiled. 'You must only ever use your magic to help people and do good things, you must never tell anyone about it or the magic will stop and go away' and with that the Wizard disappeared in a puff of purple smoke.

Bacon wasn't really interested in magic, he just wanted Tickles to play ball.

From that day on Tickles was always able to complete all of the jobs he was given, and find time to help others who were lagging behind in their work-load.

Tickles also became the smartest and tidiest soldier in the whole of the Toy Town Army.

General Basher was very pleased with him.
Sergeant Major Bullhorn was very pleased with him.
Corporal Careless was very pleased with him.
Corporal Cook was very pleased with him.
Everyone in the Toy Town Army was very
pleased with him.
Tickles was having a wonderful time.

Windows clean................................Tickle! Tickle! Atishoo!
Boots and shoes clean....................Tickle! Tickle! Atishoo!
Potatoes peel................................Tickle! Tickle! Atishoo!
Floors clean................................. Tickle! Tickle! Atishoo!
Stables clean.................................Tickle! Tickle! Atishoo!
All the jobs he had to do................. Tickle! Tickle! Atishoo!

And it was all done.....................................as if by magic.

After that Tickles really began to enjoy his magic but he often wished he could share it with someone.

The only one who knew was Tickles' best friend, Bacon the dog. Tickles never forgot the Wizard's friendly warning, 'If you tell anyone the magic will just disappear' so Tickles guarded his magic secret very carefully indeed.

One day Tickles heard a great commotion coming from the Toy Town square, even Bacon ran to the square to see what all the fuss was about.

Private Tickles rushed to find out what was happening. 'What's going on, Corporal'? he said to Corporal Careless.

Corporal Careless was just rushing past. 'The Hairies are coming' he said in a very serious voice.

Tickles knew that they had to get ready to go and stop them. One of the most important jobs of the Toy Town Army was to keep the Hairies away from Toy Town where Tickles and his friends and all the people lived. It was very hard to keep them away and they tried to invade time and time again.

The Hairies lived in the dark and dense area of the forest that surrounded the lake. It was smelly and damp.

Sometimes their hair was so long and thick that they looked like great big balls of fur but they were not at all cuddly. In fact they were mean and bad tempered. They were never satisfied and stole everything they could get their claws into.

Private Tickles rushed off to his barrack room to get ready to chase the Hairies away. He buckled on his sword and belt and his pack and then he looked in the mirror to make sure he was properly dressed and looking just right.

Tickles looked proudly at himself in the mirror. He looked very smart and soldier like. Then he went back to see Corporal Careless who was with the other soldiers in the square.

They were all lined up and ready to march away. He asked Corporal Careless where he should stand but he was told that he was too young to fight with the other soldiers. The little soldier hung his head in disappointment, and as he waved goodbye a little tear drop ran down his cheek.

Soon all the other soldiers from the Toy Town Army were there in the town square to watch and cheer as General Basher led the column of very smart soldiers away towards the forest to meet the Hairies. Everyone was there, except Private Tickles……………can you guess where he had gone?

He had run off with Bacon the dog to chase away the Hairies, running through the fields and forests as fast as he could.

Tickles raced along with Bacon, urging him to run faster.

Soon Tickles found the Hairies coming out of the forest.
Tickles just stood his ground and drew his sword.

'OK you Hairy Monsters, who's going to be first?'.

When the Hairies saw the little soldier standing his ground, with his sword raised in challenge, they all just laughed and laughed.

'Is that all that the Toy Town Army could send'?' the Hairies jeered 'He's just a young soldier and a very small one at that' said the Hairies General. He was called General Nasty Pants and nobody liked him, not even his own men, but then, nobody liked anybody in the Hairies Army.

'Hairieeeees' shouted Private Tickles, his face went bright red and his nose began to tickle and tickle and tickle more than it ever had before…………Then he sneezed the biggest and loudest sneeze he had ever sneezed …………………………
Aaaaaatishooooooooo………………..
'Hairies begone forever'………………
………………………………..and they were.

Bacon the dog lifted his head and looked up at the little soldier.
WOW!
But Tickles just smiled and said nothing.

The forest was quiet and peaceful.

The Hairies were running and tumbling away as fast as their stumpy little legs would carry them. Far away from Toy Town and Tickles and his friends. They were running back to their dark and nasty forest castle and they would never come back.

Tickles carefully put away his sword and then he started to laugh. He laughed and laughed so much that he nearly fell over. Bacon was totally confused by what he had seen and didn't understand it one little bit, but he was very happy about what his little friend had done.

Tickles then decided it was time for them to go home and he promised Bacon that he would go to the camp kitchen and find him some nice juicy bones as a treat for all his hard work. They had to be sure not to meet General Basher and the other soldiers coming the other way. It wouldn't do for the General to ask them what they'd been up to……………………….would it?

When General Basher and his soldiers arrived at the edge of the forest where the Hairies should have been, they were nowhere to be seen. The forest was quiet, peaceful and sunny. General Basher frowned and scratched his head and then puffed up his chest and spoke to his soldiers

'D'you see men, the Hairies have gone, they must have run away when they heard that it was me leading you into battle.' General Basher could be a little bit pompous at times but the soldiers didn't mind, they all liked their General very much and besides they had a nice walk back to camp in the sunshine to look forward to and they really had not been keen to meet the Hairies. 'Three cheers for General Basher' they cried. 'Hip Hip Hooray - Hip Hip Hooray - Hip Hip Hooray' and they all sat down to eat their sandwiches. It was just like having a picnic.

But we all know who the real hero is, don't we?

AAAAAtishOOOOOOOOOOOOOOO...............
'Ha!' Thought Private Tickles. 'If only I could tell someone my secret'..but he knew he wouldn't.

Perhaps Toy Town might need his help and his magic again one day.
He smiled happily. He was so sleepy. The day's excitement had made him really tired. Bacon the dog was curled up with Noodle the cat and both were fast asleep,
....and on his bed too!

Tickles put on his pyjamas, sat down on his bedside chair and 'Oh! Yaaaaawwnn' …..fell fast asleep……………,

In his castle by the lake the Wizard smiled and went to bed too. Magic is a very tiring business.

Good Night

The End.